DEDICATION:

We dedicate this book to the people of South Africa, to the preservation of African wildlife, and to the MalaMala Game Reserve, where the thrill of adventure sowed the seeds for this book.

Safari in South Africa

ADVENTURES OF RILEY™

Safari in South Africa

BY

Amanda Lumry

AND

Laura Hurwitz

ILLUSTRATED BY

Sarah McIntyre

SCHOLASTIC PRESS ★ NEW YORK

Dear Riley,

Greetings from your wild Uncle Max! We are off again on another adventure! I'm so happy that you could join me, Aunt Martha, and Cousin Alice on safari in the South African bush.

We are going to give the animal population a "checkup." We won't actually be taking their temperatures or giving them shots, but we will be counting the members of their families, especially babies, to see if their numbers are increasing or decreasing. Your parents tell me that you are good at arithmetic, so this should be a snap!

Cheers,

Uncle Max

"You're finally here!" Alice squealed, almost knocking Riley over with a bear hug.

Aunt Martha smiled. "Welcome to Johannesburg!"

"You'll barely have a chance to put your feet on the ground, Carrot Top. We have one more short flight to camp. Are you game? Sorry, bad joke," winked Uncle Max.

1

The small plane flew them far away from the city and deep into the African bush. Once they landed, two men greeted them.

"Hello, my name is Chad," said the first man. "I will be your guide, or ranger, as we are known here."

"And my name is Hendrik," said the other man. "I will be your tracker," he said, shaking Riley's hand. They headed off toward camp.

"Tracker? What's a tracker?" asked Alice.

"I watch for animals and birds, then point them out for everyone to see," said Hendrik. "Sitting up here in the vehicle helps me find them. Look! There is a lilac-breasted roller."

Lilac-Breasted Roller

➤ It gets its name from its funny, floppy way of flying.

➤ It chases and eats insects around other animals' feet.

➤ It follows fires to look for insects that have been scared away.

—Dr. Neil Burgess,
Senior Conservation
Scientist, World
Wildlife Fund

After unpacking, they ate lunch on the deck. Alice and Riley could hardly sit still.

"We're ready to start our game drive whenever you are," said Chad.

As they were loading their gear into the car, Uncle Max suddenly turned around and ran off. He quickly returned, out of breath. "I almost forgot my **GPS** unit. That's where I keep track of everything we see."

Uncle Max spoke into his tape recorder. "Testing. One . . . two . . . three! This is Professor Maxwell Plimpton. I am here in South Africa with my ace counting team. It is day one, and we are ready to go!"

Nyala

➤ A male nyala's fur changes from a reddish brown to a brown-gray with age.

➤ A male nyala sometimes fights to the death with other nyalas.

➤ A nyala will stand on its hind legs in order to reach higher branches to feed.

—Dr. Robert S. Hoffmann, Senior Scientist, Smithsonian Institution

They had not gone far when Hendrik saw some antelope. "These nyalas are only found in southern Africa."

As Uncle Max was busy entering their first sighting into his **GPS**, the antelope looked up in alarm and leaped into the bush.

"Why did they leave? Did we scare them?" asked Riley.

"No, I think there might be danger close by," Chad said.

"Ohh!" whispered Riley and Alice.

At least I got a great picture before they ran away, Riley thought to himself.

Not far from the nyalas, they came across two lively cheetah cubs.

"They seem to be playing soccer, cheetah-style," said Aunt Martha.

"Yeah! A stinky game, considering their ball is made of elephant poop!" said Chad.

"Yuck!" said Alice.

"I bet it was the cheetahs that scared the nyalas," said Riley.

"Quite likely," answered Uncle Max, "since the nyalas need to protect their young from **predators**, including cheetahs."

Cheetah

➤ It makes a chirping sound rather than a growl or roar.

➤ A cheetah has around 3,000 spots on its body.

➤ The pattern of spots on a cheetah's tail is unique, like a human fingerprint.

—Theresa Brinkcate, Manager of The Green Trust South Africa, World Wildlife Fund

On the way back to camp, Hendrik signaled Chad to stop the vehicle. There was a pack of small animals hiding in the grass.

"Look! Dogs!" said Alice.

"Yes, those are dogs, but not the kind you would have as pets. Those are African wild dogs with their pups," said Hendrik.

"What a rare treat!" said Uncle Max happily. "You see, wild dogs are becoming harder to find in South Africa as people take over the land the dogs call home."

Wild Dog

➤ It lives in groups called packs, which have two to thirty members.

➤ An adult dog feeds its young with food it chews first and then spits out.

➤ It is **endangered** because people see it as a pest and hunt it.

—Dr. Joshua Ginsberg, Director, Asia Regional Program, Wildlife Conservation Society

That night everyone yawned their way through dinner and went straight to bed.

"We sure saw a lot of babies today," said Riley sleepily.

"Yes, we did," said Uncle Max. "I was happy to see the nyalas as well as the wild dogs and the cheetahs. In nature, there needs to be a balance between **prey** and **predator**. Without a balance, neither one can survive . . ." He looked over and saw that Riley had fallen fast asleep.

They started the next morning with another game drive.
"Can I sit in the back with you today, Hendrik?" asked Riley.
"Of course," said Hendrik.
Passing through a wooded area, Alice saw
something fly over her head.

"Look!" she cried, pointing. "Monkeys! In Nepal a monkey stole my dad's underwear. Remember that, Riley?"

"I sure do!" he replied.

"Huh? How interesting," said Chad, giving them both a funny look. "These are actually *baboons*, and as far as I know, baboons don't wear any clothes."

The leaping baboons were tricky to count! Uncle Max finally finished and they moved on.

Baboon

➤ A baboon lives in groups of 50 to 200.

➤ It is an **omnivore**, which means that it eats both plants and animals.

➤ It sleeps in trees to stay safe from hyenas, lions, and other **predators.**

—Dr. Richard W. Thorington, Jr.,
Curator of Mammals,
Smithsonian Institution

➤ A mother giraffe will stand up while giving birth so it can watch for **predators**.

➤ A baby giraffe can stand up within fifteen minutes of being born.

➤ It can grow up to 18 ft. (5.5 m) high and is the tallest animal in the world.

—Jennifer D'Amico Hales,
Senior Conservation
Specialist, World Wildlife Fund

Giraffe

Hendrik motioned to them.
"Shh . . . up ahead is a mother
giraffe with her baby."

Watching the giraffes munch
made Riley hungry. He pulled
out a chocolate bar and wolfed
it down, dropping the wrapper
to the ground. He thought
nothing of it as they headed
toward the river.

On the other side of some tall reeds, a herd of elephants stood drinking.

"Look! Three babies," Alice said, counting. "They are so sweet!" A mother elephant flapped her ears and stomped toward them.

"Time to go!" said Chad. "Female elephants are very protective of their young."

"It would not take much for that elephant to push this car over," Uncle Max said nervously as they drove away.

Just then, the back tire sank into the soft mud. They were stuck, and the elephant was still hot on their trail!

"Riley, please hold this!" cried Uncle Max, handing him his tape recorder. He jumped out to help the other adults. Riley and Alice held their breath as the elephant charged closer. The earth shook with each step.

Elephant

➤ A herd is usually led by a wise old female elephant.

➤ An elephant enjoys spending time with other elephants.

➤ An adult elephant is too big for **predators**, such as lions, to bring down.

—Dr. Rob Little, Conservation Director, World Wildlife Fund, South Africa

15

Squirming in his seat, Riley dropped the tape recorder. A thunderous lion's roar echoed up and down the river. The adults froze at the sound, while the elephant turned and crashed into the reeds.

With no danger in sight, all eyes turned to a bright red Riley.

"Sorry," he said. "I dropped the tape recorder when I got scared."

"Good thing you did." Uncle Max grinned. "It seems the lion noises I taped in the Serengeti sure scared that elephant. Good job, Carrot Top!"

Black and White Rhino Differences

➤ A white rhino gets its name from its wide lips. The Afrikaans word for *wide* sounds like "white."

➤ A black rhino is usually darker than a white rhino and has a hooked upper lip.

—Eric Dinerstein, Chief Scientist, Vice President for Science, World Wildlife Fund

Soon they were all out of the mud and, hopefully, out of danger.

"Look over behind that bush!" whispered Riley. "I thought it was that grumpy elephant again, but it is a black rhino instead."

"Good sighting!" Hendrik said. "You're close, but this is really a *white* rhino and her baby. *Black* rhinos are **endangered** and really hard to find because they have been poached."

"Poached? Like an egg?" asked Alice.

"Not exactly," said Uncle Max. "Poaching is when an animal is illegally hunted and killed for its skin or horns, which are sold for a lot of money. Entire **species** have been killed off, and the black rhino could be next."

"That is so sad," Riley said.

After the sun set, they started back to camp. Hendrik whistled to Chad to slow down and aimed his spotlight at a furry little creature.

"Here we have a South African galago, also known as a bushbaby!" said Hendrik.

"I read about those in school," Riley said. "They pee on their hands and feet to help them grip tree branches when they jump and climb."

"I hope that doesn't give you any ideas!" Uncle Max chuckled.

South African Galago

➤ A galago has big eyes to help it see at night.

➤ It eats both plants and animals, but its favorite food is grasshoppers!

—Dr. Colleen McCann,
Curator of Primates,
Wildlife Conservation Society

Under the stars they
ate dinner in a *boma*,
which is a roofless hut
made of tall reeds.
Riley and Alice danced
and sang with the women
who worked at the camp.

19

After a good night's sleep, they drove to the top of a **kopje** to watch the sunrise. For breakfast, they nibbled on muffins while sipping tea and hot cocoa.

20

The car's engine began to sputter on their way down the **kopje**.

"I bet the **radiator** needs water again," said Chad.

"Let's get some from the river," suggested Hendrik.

"Can I help?" begged Riley. Hendrik nodded. Together they knelt down to fill a bottle. A mother hippo and her baby popped out of the water. The mother made a loud honking sound.

"Let's leave while we still can," said Hendrik. "I think we woke them up, and they sure sound grouchy!"

Hippopotamus

➤ The hippo kills more humans than any other African animal. When surprised, it may bite or squash its victim to reach its water hole.

➤ A hippo is a **herbivore**, which means that it does not eat meat.

➤ It spends most of the day in the water so it won't get sunburned!

—Dr. Jesus E. Maldonado, Research Geneticist, Smithsonian Institution

21

With water in the **radiator**, the vehicle ran much better. They didn't get very far because they soon met a roadblock of Cape buffalo. Riley and Alice counted ten babies. The air around them was full of bugs, swishing tails, and busy birds known as oxpeckers. Uncle Max reached into his bag to pull out his **GPS**, but was shocked to find it wasn't there!

Cape Buffalo

➤ A male Cape buffalo has horns that grow together to form a helmet.

➤ A Cape buffalo likes to roam and graze in large herds.

—Dr. Pat Thomas,
Curator of Mammalogy,
Wildlife Conservation Society

Oxpeckers help Cape buffalo by eating ticks, bugs, and ear wax, and by cleaning their open wounds.

Back at camp, everyone helped Uncle Max look for his **GPS**, but they couldn't find it. He was very upset, but a swim in the pool made him feel much better.

Chad smiled. "On such a hot day, you'd better be on the lookout for any wild animals that might want to cool off in the pool with you!"

On the afternoon game drive, Alice asked, "Are those baby leopards?"

"Great spotting, Alice!" laughed Uncle Max, poking Riley in the ribs.

One leopard started choking and coughed up a bright red object. "It's a wrapper!" Hendrik said, picking it up with a long stick.

"I dropped that yesterday! I didn't know something so small could hurt an animal," Riley said.

"Litter of any size or amount can cause a big problem. We all share this world, and we have to look out for animals," said Hendrik. Riley nodded, taking it all in.

Leopard

➤ A leopard is good at climbing trees—unlike a lion or cheetah.

➤ It hides its food in tree branches so **predators** and **scavengers** can't steal it.

➤ It hardly makes any sound at all, except a small cough to tell other animals to stay away.

—Lisa Padfield, Deputy Director of Conservation, World Wildlife Fund, South Africa

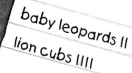

baby leopards II
lion cubs IIII

Farther down the road, Hendrik pointed to a lioness and her chubby cubs, which rolled playfully around her.

"I count four lion cubs, all healthy," said Uncle Max into his tape recorder. "A sighting like this is just what I hoped for. Seeing all of these animals tells me that their population is growing at a good rate."

He sighed, "If only I could find my **GPS** unit and record this sighting properly."

"Don't worry, Uncle Max!" said Riley. "I wrote everything down for you. See?"

Lion

➤ A lioness lives with other lionesses in prides with their young.

➤ A lioness will frequently do the food hunting, but it is the lion that eats first. The lioness eats second, followed by the young.

—Dr. Graeme Patterson, Assistant Director, Africa Regional Program, Wildlife Conservation Society

Hendrik whistled quietly. "I don't believe my eyes."

"Is that what I think it is?" asked Chad.

"Yes," said Hendrik. "A black rhino! We have not seen one here in years."

"It has a wound on its side, probably caused by a poacher's bullet," Uncle Max said, shaking his head. "This rhino was lucky to have gotten away."

Chad radioed the news to the camp.

As they were leaving, Riley nudged Alice. "Look at that! I only dropped a little wrapper, but that piece of litter is so big a lion could choke on it."

Uncle Max whooped, "Riley! That's my **GPS**! It must have fallen out last night when we were on our way back to camp!"

Black Rhino

➤ It is hunted because its horns are wanted for traditional Asian medicine.

➤ Since 1960, poaching has reduced its population from 100,000 down to just 3,725.

—Dr. George Amato, Director, Science Resource Center, Wildlife Conservation Society

That night,
Riley dreamed
of Africa.

28

Uncle Max woke Riley up in the morning. "I am so glad that you found my **GPS**, Carrot Top. You saved the day, and maybe some animals as well. The animal population here is strong, but poaching is still a big problem," he said, speedily typing away. He finally looked up. "Let's go eat! I'm as hungry as a lion!"

At the table, Chad said, "I thought you would like to know we received a report. The black rhino was spotted heading into Mozambique."

"I wish we could follow it," Alice said.

"These journeys are a lot easier for animals, since they don't have to make travel plans and get passports," said Uncle Max. "It is up to the governments to allow them to move freely so they can find food and other herds."

29

They headed to the airstrip. "Thanks for letting me sit with you!" Riley said, giving Hendrik a hug. "I wish I could be a tracker when I grow up."

"You would make a fine one!" Hendrik told Riley, handing him a brimmed hat just like his. "This is for you, so you can practice your tracking skills."

Back at home, Riley entertained his family with stories of the African bush, Hendrik and Chad, the angry elephant, and the mysterious black rhino. His hat proved to be very helpful in tracking neighborhood pets as he returned to living the life of a nine-year-old . . . until the mail arrived with a new letter from Uncle Max.

Where will Riley go next?

FURTHER INFORMATION

Glossary

endangered: something that is at risk of being lost forever

GPS (Global Positioning System): an instrument that uses radio signals and satellites to show someone's exact position on earth

herbivore: an animal that only eats plants

kopje (KOP-pee): a small hill made of rocks

omnivore: an animal that eats both plants and other animals

predator: an animal that kills and eats smaller and weaker animals

prey: a smaller or weaker animal that has to run quickly or it will become a predator's meal

radiator: a device in a car usually filled with water that keeps the engine cool

scavenger: an animal that steals or eats other animals' prey

species: different kinds of plants and animals

survive: to continue to live

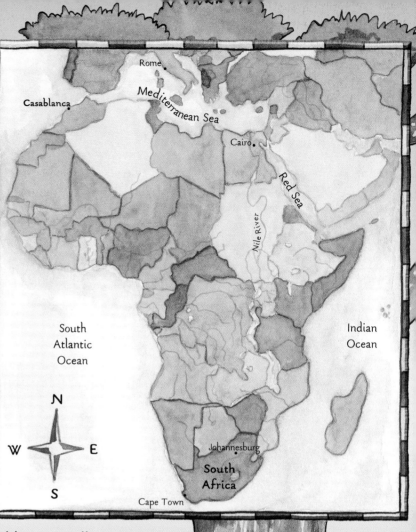

Guns to Cameras

Over the past fifty years, the main visitors to Africa's private game reserves have changed from hunters to photographers. This new interest in preserving animals and their native habitats has helped Africa's landscapes and animal populations thrive. One of the first reserves to make this change was the MalaMala Game Reserve in South Africa, under the guidance of its owners, the Rattray family. MalaMala is a very special place, and many of the photographs in this book were taken there.

JOIN US FOR MORE GREAT ADVENTURES!

RILEY'S WORLD

Visit our website at
www.adventuresofriley.com

to find out how
you can join Riley's
super kids' club!

ADVENTURES OF RILEY™

Look for these other
great Riley books:

➤ Project Panda
➤ Polar Bear Puzzle
➤ South Pole Penguins

A special thank-you to all the scientists who collaborated on this project. Your time and assistance are very much appreciated.

First published in China in 2003 by Eaglemont Press.
www.eaglemont.com

All photographs by Amanda Lumry except:
Page 8 wild dogs and page 18 South African galago © Paul Funston
Page 27 black rhino © Gerald Hinde

Illustrations © 2003 by Sarah McIntyre
Additional Illustrations and Layouts by Ulkutay & Ulkutay, London WC2E 9RZ
Editing and Digital Compositing by Michael E. Penman
Digital Imaging by Embassy Graphics, Canada and Phoenix Color

Library of Congress Control Number: 2003105372

ISBN-13: 978-0-545-06827-7
ISBN-10: 0-545-06827-4

10 9 8 7 6 5 4 3 2 1   08 09 10 11 12

Printed in Mexico   49
First Scholastic printing, June 2008

A portion of the proceeds from your purchase of this licensed product supports the stated educational mission of the Smithsonian Institution — "the increase and diffusion of knowledge." The name of the Smithsonian Institution and the sunburst logo are registered trademarks of the Smithsonian Institution and are registered in the U.S. Patent and Trademark Office. www.si.edu

2% of the proceeds from this book will be donated to the Wildlife Conservation Society. http://wcs.org

An average royalty of approximately 3 cents from the sale of each book in the Adventures of Riley series will be received by World Wildlife Fund (WWF) to support their international efforts to protect endangered species and their habitats. ® WWF Registered Trademark Panda Symbol © 1986 WWF. © 1986 Panda symbol WWF-World Wide Fund For Nature (also known as World Wildlife Fund) ® "WWF" is a WWF Registered Trademark © 1986 WWF-Fonds Mondial pour la Nature symbole du panda Marque Déposée du WWF ®

We try to produce the most beautiful books possible and we are extremely concerned about the impact of our manufacturing process on the forests of the world and the environment as a whole. Accordingly, we made sure that the paper used in this book has been certified as coming from forests that are managed to ensure the protection of the people and wildlife dependent upon them.